POLLY'S CHRISTMAS PRESENT

(The Christmas Puppy)

Story and Pictures by IRMA WILDE

WONDER BOOKS • NEW YORK

A Division of GROSSET & DUNLAP, Inc.

"OH DEAR, oh dear, oh dear me!" cried Santa Claus.
"What *am* I going to do?"

"Fuss, fuss, fuss," scolded Mrs. Santa Claus, hurrying into Santa's workroom. "Whatever are you fussing about? Haven't you just finished ten little toy dogs? There's one for Billy, Bobby and Dick, Tommy, Tim, Mickey, Larry and Nick. And one for each twin, Neddy and Eddy. I'm sure that is all you have to do."

"All indeed!" said Santa Claus. "Here is a letter from Polly, and she wants a toy dog too!

"Tonight is Christmas Eve, and I must do my yearly visiting. I haven't time to make another toy dog. Oh dear, oh dear me! I don't want to disappoint Polly."

"That *is* too bad," said Mrs. Santa. "But Polly should have written to you earlier. I guess she will just have to be disappointed.

"It's time for you to go. All the reindeer are hitched up to the sleigh and waiting outside. Put on your boots and your cap and coat. I'll finish packing your bag."

Santa Claus felt very sad as he put on his warm coat. He had never disappointed a little girl or boy before. Santa Claus looked down at his own dog, Jingle, and suddenly he had a wonderful idea!

"Why, Mrs. Santa Claus," he said, "Jingle's puppies are old enough to leave their mother now. Do you think Polly would like a real live puppy instead of a little toy dog?"

"I'm sure she would!" said Mrs. Santa. "How smart you are, Santa, to think of such a wonderful surprise for Polly. Now, which one shall we give her?"

Santa and Mrs. Santa hurried over to the basket where Jingle's puppies were playing. There were three puppies in the basket — a brown puppy, a brown-and-white puppy and a black-and-white puppy.

"I think Polly would like the black-and-white puppy, Santa," said Mrs. Santa.

"Well, well," said Santa Claus to the little puppy, "you're going to have a new home. And you will have a little girl named Polly to take care of you."

The little puppy gave a tiny happy bark and wagged his little black tail.

Santa tucked the puppy inside his great red coat to keep him warm. Then he climbed into his sleigh.

Off into the sky went Santa Claus and his reindeer!
"Ha, ha, ha and a ho, ho, ho," laughed Santa as his
reindeer flew across the sky with the sleigh full of toys.

Santa visited all the children. He stopped off at Billy's, Bobby's and Dick's houses, and all the other boys' houses. And Amy's and Judy's and Nancy's houses and all the other girls' houses. And he stopped at Polly's house, too.

Much later, just as dawn was about to lighten the sky, Santa Claus turned toward home again. He was very happy, and he laughed and he sang and he winked at his reindeer. Santa knew that there would be a lot of happy children on Christmas day!

Christmas morning, Polly was the first one down-stairs at her house.

She tiptoed down the stairs, through the hall and peeped into the living room.

There was the tree all shining and bright, with tinsel and gaily colored decorations.

There were the packages beautifully wrapped and holding lovely secrets.

And there was Polly's Christmas stocking! "My little toy dog!" cried Polly. "The little toy dog I asked Santa to bring! It's here! It's here! It's in my stocking!"

She took down the stocking and lifted out the tiny dog! And then she heard a tiny bark!

"Oh!" cried Polly. "Why, you're a real *live* puppy dog! You're warm and cuddly and I love you! I never saw such a darling little puppy. I will name you Inky."

The little puppy barked happily and wagged his tail as hard as he could!

"I wish you could tell me how you got into my Christmas stocking, Inky! Did Santa Claus bring you?" asked Polly.

But Inky just smiled a happy puppy-dog smile. He snuggled closer to Polly and kissed her cheek.

Inky would never tell Polly how it happened that he came to live with her!

It was a lovely Christmas for Polly and Inky. Polly got her Christmas wish, and Inky had a little girl to take care of him, and play with him, and love him.